REDCOATS AND PETTICOATS

by Katherine Kirkpatrick
illustrated by Ronald Himler

Holiday House / New York

For my mother, Audrey,
and my sister, Jennifer,
and for the next generation:
Alexander, Nicholas, and Alice

Text copyright © 1999 by Katherine Anne Kirkpatrick
Illustrations copyright © 1999 by Ron Himler, Inc.
ALL RIGHTS RESERVED
Printed in the United States of America
FIRST EDITION

Library of Congress Cataloging-in-Publication Data
Kirkpatrick, Katherine.
Redcoats and petticoats / by Katherine Kirkpatrick; illustrated
by Ronald Himler. — 1st ed.
p.   cm.
Includes bibliographical references (p.   )
Summary: Members of a family in the village of Setauket on Long
Island are displaced by the Redcoats and serve as spies for the
Revolutionary Army of George Washington.
ISBN 0-8234-1416-7 (reinforced)
1. New York (State)—History—Revolution, 1775–1783—Juvenile
fiction. [1. New York (State)—History—Revolution, 1775–1783—
Fiction. 2. United States—History—Revolution, 1775–1783
—Fiction. 3. Spies—Fiction. 4. Setauket (N.Y.)—Fiction.]
I. Himler, Ronald, ill. II. Title.
PZ7.K6354Rg   1999   98-15450   CIP   AC
[Fic]—dc21

When the war came to our village of Setauket, Long Island, the Redcoats made our church into a fort. Cannon balls whistled through the air. The Village Green was alive with hurrying people. The worst was soon to come.

One night there was a loud rapping on our door. Two Redcoats flung open the door and grabbed my father. "Traitor!" I heard one of them say, holding a musket to his head.

Father called to me as the Redcoats took him away. "Thomas, help your mother to take care of the family."

The next day a company of Redcoats moved into our house. They sat on our chairs and slept in our beds. Noisy voices came at us from every direction. Mother's eyes grew fiery when a tall soldier, sitting at our table, licked his fingers as he finished gnawing on a chicken bone. "That was our dinner!" she scolded.

My mother's parents, Grandmother Martha and Grandfather Tangier Smith, urged us to come live with them. Mother refused. "These things wouldn't be happening to your family if you remained loyal to our king," Grandfather said.

"I'm sorry, but I have my principles," Mother argued.

Our family moved nearby to a little cottage on the water, across from Abraham Woodhull's farm. "What's living in a big house? We'll have it back when the war ends," Mother told me.

Soon after that Mother started to do odd things. "Thomas, take your row-boat and go out to Conscience Bay. See if you can find a whaleboat any-where about."

"Why?" I asked.

Mother refused to answer. Instead, she hummed to herself as she washed my sisters' red petticoats in a wooden basin. "Don't forget your fishing pole!" she added.

Conscience Bay was a long way to row just to go fishing. Was Mother becoming touched in the head?

I rowed along the narrow, marshy beaches, hugging close to the shore-line. A few schooners were sailing in the harbor that day, as well as many smaller vessels. I looked up on a hill and saw, above the trees, the fires of a camp. Then I noticed small figures in the distance. They were wearing red!

As I drifted back to the bank, I saw the Redcoats watching me. I quickened my strokes and rowed through a narrow channel into Conscience Bay. The coves wove in and out of the shore like fingers on a hand. There was no whaleboat in sight. I had made my long trip for nothing!

When I returned home after passing the Redcoats a second time, Mother asked me, "Did you see the whaleboat?"

"No, I did not. But I saw the Redcoats' camp on the shore!"

"Oh, those scoundrels! They're everywhere! Tomorrow I'd like you to return to the Bay to look for the whaleboat."

"But Mother, I don't see why," I protested. I did not want to admit I was afraid.

Mother looked up from hanging my sisters' red petticoats on the line. She gave me a look that meant she was serious. "You are helping your father," she said. "If you see the Redcoats again, why don't you wave to them?"

The next day I brought my brother Ben with me. While we caught enough bluefish for our family's supper, I wondered how my search for a whaleboat could possibly help my father. I wondered where the Redcoats had taken him.

On the return trip home, we passed by the Redcoats' camp. There were more soldiers than I had ever seen before at one time. A group of five walked toward the beach. They carried muskets.

"You boys, what are you doing there?" a tall Redcoat called. It was the same tall Redcoat who lived in my old house.

I was too frightened to speak. Instead, I waved to him as we rowed by.

"Did you see the whaleboat, boys?" Mother asked expectantly.

"No," I answered. I was angry. "There are Redcoats all over the shore. I can't go out to Conscience Bay without rowing past them! I wish you would tell me what's happening."

Mother sighed. "Sometimes it's not safe for me to tell you everything," she said as she hugged me. "You're a brave boy, Thomas, and I know your father would be proud of you," she added. Then she hung her red petticoats on the line.

"Why are you doing so much wash?" I asked.

"Oh . . . There's always wash to be done," Mother answered vaguely. I saw that one of the petticoats Mother was hanging was actually dry. The war was surely affecting her.

The following morning Mother sent me out to look for the whaleboat again. I approached the Redcoats' camp, keeping under cover of the trees as long as I could. The tall Redcoat was there, along with several companions. "Boy, come here!" he said. His face was round and ruddy under his high hat.

I was just a few strokes from the beach.

"What have we here? Clams! I'd like some clams for my lunch. Bring them up to us!" another Redcoat called out.

Carrying the bucket of clams, I climbed the hill to the camp. I stood in the center of the hill, surrounded by soldiers in bright red uniforms. I breathed hard.

"Should we arrest him?" the tall Redcoat asked, then laughed wildly. He took my bucket of clams. "Go on with you. Bring us some bluefish next time."

As I rounded the corner of the cove toward Conscience Bay, I saw the slender whaleboat in the shallows ahead of me. It was no ordinary whaleboat. At the bow a man in a three-pointed hat operated a swivel gun. The whaleboat held Patriot soldiers! My whole body trembling, I rowed home as fast as my boat could take me.

"Mother! Mother! I saw the whaleboat!" I called out. I ran, stumbling, toward her. Mother's eyes brightened. She embraced me, pressing her cheek against mine. "Keep your voice low," she said gently. She asked me to tell her exactly where I had seen the whaleboat.

Mother hung her black petticoat on the clothesline. I helped her hang the handkerchiefs. "Only three handkerchiefs today, Thomas," she said.

I looked at her.

"Don't ask questions," she said.

A gust of wind rose up from the Sound. The petticoat on the clothesline made a loud flapping noise as the wind tossed it back and forth.

I made many trips to Conscience Bay that summer, by boat in fair weather, and by foot when it rained. Sometimes I spotted the whaleboat, sometimes not. Whenever the tall Redcoat saw me, I had to give him all my fish. Mother continued to do the laundry. As the weeks passed, I began to doubt that Father would ever come home.

My brothers and sisters and I loaded armfuls of corn, beans, turnips, squash, and potatoes into our family's wagon. "What are we doing with these?" I asked.

"You'll see," Mother replied. "Aren't we fortunate the Redcoats haven't come by to take them? These vegetables are very valuable, Thomas. Because of the war, there are many people who haven't seen vegetables in over a year."

The road was muddy and rutted. Sometimes I rode on horseback. Sometimes I followed the cart on foot. We ate potatoes for our supper and slept with our shoes on in the wagon's soft hay. I lay awake listening to the chirping of crickets and an occasional gunshot.

"Where are we going?" I asked Mother.

"To find your father," she answered.

After three days Mother and I arrived at New York Harbor. The seas were high and choppy. The *Jersey* prison ship appeared as a dark, ugly hulk.

Redcoats approached us, carrying muskets. Chin high, Mother talked to their officer and handed him her letter. She smiled at him flirtatiously.

"This woman has influential Tory family members," the officer murmured after reading the letter. The officer called to his men to load the vegetables into one of the supply boats.

The supply boat took the officer and the vegetables out to the *Jersey*. I could smell the rotten stench from the prison ship. Squatting men, gaunt as skeletons, were scrubbing its deck. Mother and I waited anxiously. When the boat returned, Father was in it. My father had been traded for the vegetables.

"Father!" I called out. He was pale and dressed in rags, but he was still Father. He broke into a big grin when he saw me. I knew everything was going to be all right.

Father returned to our family, but only for a short time. The tall Redcoat and two of his companions came to our cottage looking for him. Father heard the sound of their horses, ran down to the beach, and hid in the tall marsh grass. Mother stood up straight, unafraid, while the Redcoats searched our cottage. I had never been so frightened.

The next day Father and I rowed together to Conscience Bay, where the whaleboat was waiting for him. "Thomas, I'm going to Connecticut until the war ends," he told me. I felt so sad that I couldn't say good-bye to him.

When next I saw Father, I was as tall as he was. I was no longer a boy. The war ended and, at last, Father came home to stay. We moved back into our old house, and we were happy to be together again as a family. To celebrate the Redcoats' departure, the people of Setauket gathered on the Village Green and roasted an ox.

Later George Washington toured Long Island. I met him when he stopped in our village. He bowed to Mother and said, "I've come here to thank you spies who have helped us to win the war."

I was shocked.

"I couldn't have done it without the help of my son Thomas," she said.

"What? A spy? How?" I asked.

"A whaleboat took secret messages across the Sound to Connecticut, where General Washington was," she said. "I signaled the location of the whaleboat to another spy, Abraham Woodhull. But the whaleboat wasn't always hidden in the same place. I had to know its whereabouts. That's where you came in, Thomas."

"What was your signal?" asked George Washington.

Mother smiled. She wouldn't answer. She liked to hold her secrets close. But *I* knew. It was her petticoats.

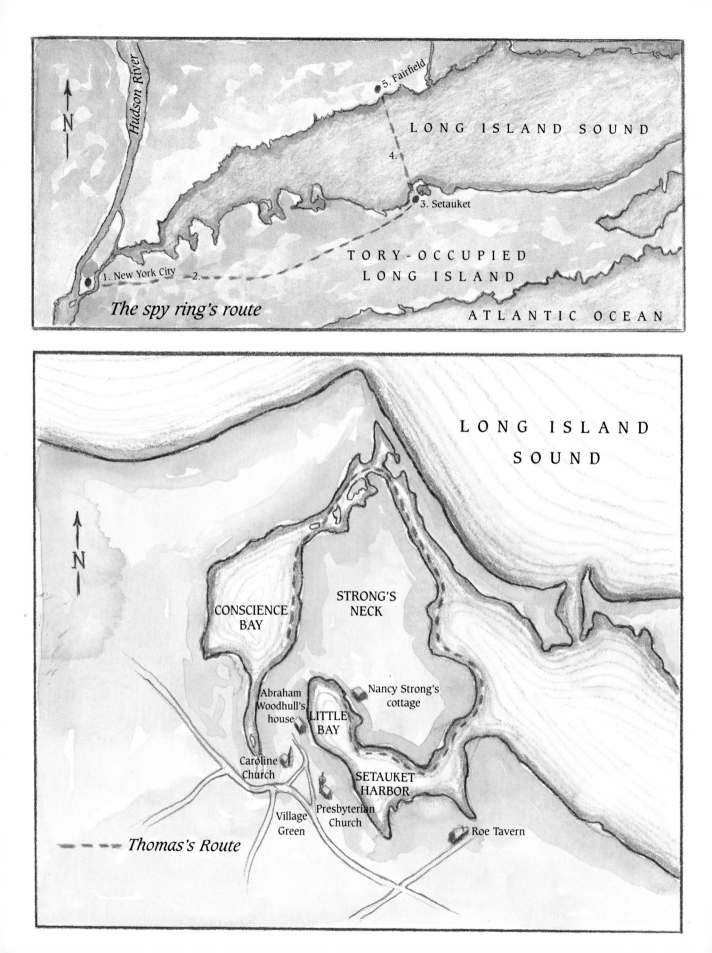

The spy ring's route

1. New York City 2. 3. Setauket 4. 5. Fairfield

Hudson River

LONG ISLAND SOUND

TORY-OCCUPIED LONG ISLAND

ATLANTIC OCEAN

N

LONG ISLAND SOUND

CONSCIENCE BAY

STRONG'S NECK

Nancy Strong's cottage

Abraham Woodhull's house

LITTLE BAY

Caroline Church

SETAUKET HARBOR

Presbyterian Church

Village Green

Roe Tavern

Thomas's Route

N

George Washington's Spies in Action

Nancy Strong's clothesline was one link in a spy chain that provided George Washington with valuable information about the British and their battle plans. This information helped the Patriots win the Revolutionary War.

1. Robert Townsend, disguised as a Redcoat, talks to the British generals in a tea room in New York City. He writes a letter to George Washington using invisible ink.

2. Setauket innkeeper, Austin Roe, gallops on horseback to New York City to pick up supplies. At the same time, he collects the letter. Back in Setauket, he hides the letter in a hollow tree on the edge of farmer Abraham Woodhull's field.

3. Nancy Strong uses her clothesline to show Abraham Woodhull the whereabouts of Caleb Brewster's whaleboat. She hangs a black petticoat as a sign that the whaleboat has arrived. Brewster has six landing spots. The number of handkerchiefs on the line indicates his location.

4. Abraham Woodhull collects the letter from the hollow tree and brings it to Caleb Brewster in his whaleboat. Caleb Brewster and his men row across Long Island Sound to Fairfield, Connecticut.

5. Major Benjamin Tallmadge delivers the letter to General George Washington.

Historical Notes

Redcoats and Petticoats is based on a true story of the people of Setauket, a little town on the north shore of Long Island, about sixty miles east of New York City. The British took the colony of New York early in the war in 1776. British soldiers, known as "Redcoats," remained encamped on Long Island for seven years. In Setauket, the Redcoats made the Presbyterian Church on the Village Green into a fort, knocking down the pews to make room for the horses and pulling out the tombstones in the churchyard to use for barricades. The Battle of Setauket occurred on August 22, 1777, when a fleet of Patriot soldiers in whaleboats came over from Connecticut in a failed attempt to take over the fort.

The Setauket Spy Ring began in 1778 and operated for six years. The spies were never found out by the British soldiers. In fact, their identities were kept a secret for over one-hundred fifty years, until the historian Morton Pennypacker broke their code. He published his findings in his 1939 book, *George Washington's Spies on Long Island and in New York*. The majority of the letters in the Spy Ring were written by Abraham Woodhull, under the alias "Samuel Culper, Sr.," and Robert Townsend from Oyster Bay, under the alias "Samuel Culper, Jr." One of the most important bits of spy work done by the Spy Ring related to the traitor Benedict Arnold. Through the efforts of the Setauket spies, the Patriots were able to capture (and execute) the important British officer Major John Andres, who, disguised in civilian clothing, was on his way to talk to Benedict Arnold. Because of Major Andres's capture, Benedict Arnold was never able to complete his plan to turn over West Point to the British.

Nancy Strong, the clothesline heroine, and her husband, Judge Selah Strong, had eight children: Keturah (b. 1761); Thomas (b. 1765); Margaret (b. 1768); Benjamin (b. 1770); Mary (died young); William (b. 1775); Joseph (b. 1777); and George Washington Strong (b. 1783). These children may or may not have been involved with the Spy Ring; some artistic liberty has been taken for the sake of the story. The particulars of why Selah Strong was captured and put on the infamous *Jersey* prison ship are not known; only that he was released in exchange for food through the efforts of his wife, who was possibly helped by Loyalist or "Tory" relatives on Long Island. After his release, Selah Strong fled to Connecticut for the duration of the war.

The *Jersey* was stationed in Wallabout Bay, site of the present Brooklyn Navy Yard. It housed about a thousand prisoners at one time, most of them captured seamen. Yellow fever was so prevalent on the ship that it became known in Revolutionary War times as the "Jersey fever"; smallpox was another of the ship's big killers. An estimated eleven thousand men died on the *Jersey*, and their bones were eventually taken to be buried under the Prison Ship Martyr's Monument in Brooklyn's Fort Greene Park.

Thomas Shepherd Strong, the thirteen-year-old hero of this story, grew up to become a judge like his father and married a local girl named Hannah Brewster. Thomas had a son named Selah Brewster Strong, who was the father of another Selah Brewster Strong, who in turn was the father of Kate Strong. Kate Strong, as a very old, blind woman over ninety, first told the story of Nancy's clothesline to me when I was a fourth grader working on a school essay. The essay won a prize from the Anna Smith Strong chapter of the Daughters of the American Revolution.

Visitors to Long Island's north shore may enjoy seeing the places featured in this story: the Village Green in Setauket, flanked by its two Revolutionary War era churches, the Caroline Church and the Setauket Presbyterian Church, and Strong's Neck, where the spy activities took place. For more information about the spies, contact the Three Village Historical Society in East Setauket. In Oyster Bay, Revolutionary War spy Robert Townsend's home is now open as a museum, Raynham Hall.